Edition Paashaas Verlag

AF280454

For Anny ...

EPV

The published recommendations in this book were carefully developed and reviewed by the author. However, a guarantee cannot be made; the author or publisher and their representatives cannot be held liable for damages to people, property or capital. Names, characters, businesses, places, events and incidents are either the products of the author's imagination or used in a fictitious manner. Any resemblance to actual persons, living or dead, or actual events are unintentional and purely coincidental.

Murder Mystery Party 1

The Bet

Author: Cornelia H.-Müller
Cover-Motive: Pixabay.de
Cover designed by Michael Frädrich
© Edition Paashaas Verlag, www.verlag-epv.de
ISBN: 978-3-96174-000-0
Printed: BoD, Norderstedt
New Edition Januar 2017
Translated from German to English by Annette Oppenlander,
Bloomington, Indiana, USA

The German National Library records this publication in the
German National Bibliography; detailed bibliographic data is
available via the Internet at http://dnb.d-nb.de

Table of Contents

Introduction

With the help of this book, you, your family and guests can search for the killer at home. Immerse yourself in an exciting murder mystery, investigate, question and evaluate facts and testimonies.

None of the participants are required to have acting skills. You and your fellow players sit together in comfort and try jointly to detect the murderer!

For this murder mystery a story of the crime exists and is read to the players, detailing what happened. Also included are descriptions of parts for all players as well as a conclusive resolution.

The murder mystery allows you to investigate at any location. Whether you and your guests try to solve the crime in your living room or outdoors during a barbecue is irrelevant.

The book works in conjunction with the Internet. You can easily download and print the required accessories. Invitations, nametags, short descriptions and roll play texts can be found at: http://www.verlag-epv.de under Downloads Krimiparty.

Your login information is as follows:
Login ID: murdermystery1
Password: hmueller17

How a Murder Mystery Works!

Instructions

Please read the main story and all complementing roll play texts thoroughly. Determine which player should take which part. It is no problem if a female player takes a male role or vice versa. However, if you would like to include yourself and investigate without knowledge of the murderer, distribute each part anonymously and under no circumstances read the resolution. This way you as the host can also work as a 'real' investigator.

Do you have Internet? If so, you can download and print the individual roll play parts for your guests at www.verlag-epv.de. If not, simply copy them from the book.

The roll play parts consist of 2 pages: the introductory text and the secret clues. We recommend distributing the roll play parts to participants on the evening of the game and not before.

If your guests are supposed to appear to the mystery evening in costume, send the introductory roll play parts along with the invitations. But please remind participants to bring along their texts to the game evening. The secret clues will definitely only be distributed on the evening of the game.

Prepare nametags with the roll play parts your guests assume. Players will attach these with tape or a safety pin for everyone to see. These are also available for download on the Internet.

Print a short description for every guest to simplify getting started, which also reminds each player about their role and name.

Game Rules

Your guests are surely already excited about what to expect. Here are a few tips on how to make your mystery evening even more successful:

Create a cozy, comfortable atmosphere and avoid harsh lights. Set out candles or small lights—this creates the right framework. Please prepare paper and pen for every guest. Notes about the story and each player's testimony are important tools during the investigation. Also have copies of the brief story summary available for your guests.

Do you have a dinner planned for your guests?

If you serve a meal with several courses, proceed as follows:

Before the appetizer, distribute the nametags. Every guest knows now, which role he'll be playing tonight.

Read the main story after the appetizer. It is noted within the story, when the action should be interrupted to enjoy the main couse. This way your evening becomes a real mystery dinner.

Afterwards, every guest receives his personal roll play part, which consists of introductory text and hints (secret text). Partipants will now discreetly study their texts. When all guests have read their parts and are ready, the introductory round begins. All players read their introductory texts in order.

The secret text includes additional information and supplements the story—this text is not read, but offers background knowledge which every player needs to investigate and can introduce into the investigation according to their own preference. The murderer also learns in his secret text that he is the perpetrator.

The investigation starts after the introductory round—introductory and secret texts generate many questions, which can now be asked and answered. Remind your guests that only the killer may lie. All others must orient themselves near the truth.

Once the investigation concludes, distribute notepaper. Every player can write down his name and who he suspects. Collect all notes. Afterwards, if it is so planned, serve dessert.

At last you as the host read the resolution of the case. Only now should the killer come forward! Based on the collected notes, share how many players determined the correct killer—potentially create a lottery to hand out prizes. That surely creates additional entertainment. The closing remarks provide the humorous ending for the evening.

If you only plan a small snack instead of a dinner, proceed as follows:

- Welcome guests and distribute nametags and short descriptions

- Distribute paper and pens for taking notes

- Read aloud main story

- Distribute individual roll play texts

- Discreet study of texts

- Introductory Round

- Investigation begins

- Guests write down suspect(s)

- Read aloud the resolution

- Announce who guessed correctly—and if so planned, draw (lottery/prize) winner

- Read closing remarks

FAQ:

Question: Does the murderer know he is the perpetrator?
Answer: Yes, this is clearly described in his secret roll play text.

Question: Are guests allowed to bend the truth or fib?
Answer: Only the killer is permitted to lie. All other players should remain close to the truth.

Question: I have more guests than parts. What now?
Answer: In the story we have created so-called guest parts. When it says: 7-10 players, there are 7 larger parts and 3 smaller guest parts. The larger parts are required, the smaller parts may be cast.

If you should have twice the number of guests, you could play at 2 tables simultaneously. Prepare parts and accessories twice, read the story from a central location and afterwards investigate at 2 tables. You'll see that this also works seamlessly. Both tables will likely arrive at different results; it depends a lot on how the individual players act.

Question: Do guests have to be of similar age?
Answer: No. During test rounds we've played with participants of various ages and mixed genders. Our players were between 16 and 80 years old, and all very much enjoyed it!

Question: Do you have to share all of the main text?
Answer: Yes, the text in the introductory round is prepared in such a way, that it provides important information, without which the investigation quickly becomes boring.

Question: My question is not listed; I need help.

Answer:

Please contact the author at <u>glashauskrimi@glashauskrimi.de</u>. She'll be happy to answer your questions for a successful murder mystery party.

Invitation

If you would like to extend a written invitation to your guests, you could use this text as an example. On the Internet you will find a prepared invitation to print out.

Invitation to a Murder Mystery Party.

Crime Scene:

_____

The investigation starts on _____

At   _____ o'clock

Please join us for an exciting evening including refreshments. As we have to indeed solve a murder, we're looking forward to an exciting time. Of course, we need your help.

Please remember to bring your reading glasses since you will receive access to classified files.

I/We would love you to join us.

Best wishes,

Please RSVP via telephone at

_____

Introductory Description of THE BET (For Planning)
A murder mystery for 7-11 people

The players are:

George, Lord Ashtenburry (58)
Lady Marjorie Ashtenburry (56)
Arthur Smith, Attorney (52)
Meril Smith, Daughter of Arthur (18)
Carol Rowney (54), Wife of Carl
Susan Rowney (34), Daughter
Ted McDonald, Businessman (30)
Vinni McCloster, Cook
Inspector Hannibal Winter
Sergeant David Mulley
Observer

Introduction
Due to a turbulent stock market Lord George Ashtenburry had to sell his Scottish manor, the venerable Linley Castle. The new owner is Carl Rowney, a Texan oil billionaire. He invites the Ashtenburrys and additional guests for dinner at the castle.

For Thomas Banister these are no easy times. As butler of the manor, who served Lord and Lady Ashtenburry diligently for many years, his services were included in the purchase. Nonetheless, everything appears to point to a jolly evening, until Carl Rowney and Lord Ashtenburry place a ludicrous bet.

Before midnight there is a corpse and Inspector Hannibal Winter will be struggling to elicit secrets from all those present and solve the murder.

A final word about the game rules:
All players should orient themselves close to the truth; only the killer may lie. However, he has to be careful because if he's caught lying, nobody will believe him anymore!
I wish you much enjoyment and murderous fun!
Cornelia H.-Müller

Distribution of Roll Play Parts
This murder mystery is suitable for about 8-11 people.
For 7 people without Hannibal, Vinni and Mulley
For 8 people without Hannibal Winter
For 9 people with Vinni
For 10 people with Mulley
For 11 people with Observer

If Hannibal doesn't participate:
Hannibal Winter's text definitely has to be read aloud in the introductory round; he introduces additional important hints. Provide Hannibal's text to Meril; she can share this knowledge throughout the evening.

Main Story to Read Aloud
The Bet!

Introductory Text

"Oh my God, what *is* that?" Horror was written on Lady Marjorie Ashtenburry's face as they rode the long driveway toward Linley-Castle. "Stop at once, George?" Her voice almost cracked with agitation.

Lord George Ashtenburry stomped the breaks of the old Rolls Royce, a remainder from better times.

From afar, they viewed the splendid portal of Linley-Castle, their former home.

Left and right of the massive entry door American flags waived. On top of the tower another star spangled banner flapped in the wind.

However, Lady Ashtenburry's gaze didn't focus on the flags, but on a strange object, which had been erected smack in the middle in front of the portal. Where a beautiful historic fountain from the 16th century had adorned the estate a few weeks earlier, stood now, in the center of a blown-up air pillow, a bizarre object with a saddle on top.

"What in the world is that?" whispered Marjorie.

"Well, I think it is called a mechanic bull!" stated the Lord in a hoarse voice.

"Mechanic bull? Here…in front of the castle? What do you do with it and where…where is the fountain?"

"One rides a mechanic bull! One sits on top, it moves, more or less fiercely depending on the setting, and one tries to remain on top as long as possible."

"I don't understand." Marjorie appeared confused. "Don't they have horses?"

"It is more likely a type of sport, my dear."

"And where is the fountain? Did he tear it down?"

"Looks like it."

Ashtenburry restarted the engine and drove slowly to the front of the portal. Indeed, the mechanic bull sat exactly in the spot, where the ornate fountain with statues, built by an ancestor of the Ashtenburrys, had previously resided.

For a while the Lord and Lady remained silent.

"It is none of our business," stated George with a firm voice. "He owns the castle and he can do with it what he wants."

"Unfortunately, he can," said Marjorie. "And it is also unfortunate that we had to accept this invitation. I wish, the evening were over already."

The Lord sighed deeply. "You know I have my reasons. And now…let us go inside."

Carl Rowney, as always dressed in a checkered shirt, pointed western boots and a cowboy hat, entered the large wine cellar in the old walls of Linley Castle and tried the black light switch several times. The front vault remained dark, only beyond, in the second vault, a neon tube sprang to life and created enough light.

"Hmm," grumbled Rowney and turned to Banister, his butler, who stood right behind him. "The light is broken here upfront. Fletcher needs to take a look at it tomorrow."

Banister nodded.

Rowney grunted contentedly and marched farther into the back, the part of the cellar now lit and proudly examined his assets. He'd bought the estate including personal property and he particularly enjoyed the wine cellar. It stretched across two large vaults of 200 square meters. A good 2,000 bottles of the best wine and premium champaign were shelved in more than 50 wine racks.

Rowney patted Erwin, his German shepherd's head, lit a cigar and puffed out a smoke cloud with relish. Then he proudly marched past the shelves. Occasionally, he stopped, pulled one of the dusty bottles from a shelf and read the label.

"And, Banister," he asked turning toward his butler, who had followed at a suitable distance, "what will we serve our guests for the celebration?"

Lowering his gaze, Banister took a step closer.

"Well, Sir, Mrs. McCloster will serve clear oxtail soup with parsley as a first course. I would recommend a light sparkling wine. Since it has to be cold, I have already taken the liberty this morning to place a sparkling wine of the Shiraz-varietal in the cooler."

Rowney took a step closer. "And, what will it do?"

Banister tilted his head. "This vintage is uncomplicated and approachable. Its aromas of plum, licorice and white pepper are captivating, to say the least. It tickles the throat and creates a desire for more."

"Ha!" Rowney's laughter echoed through the vault. "Wonderful, Banister, simply wonderful. His lordship will be duly impressed, right?"

"Well," said Banister, "Lord Ashtenburry bought this sparkling wine at an auction in 2009. I assume he still remembers this wine and will be very pleased he can enjoy it here today."

"And what will we take with the main course?"

Banister didn't wait long with an answer.

"Since we will have wild game as the main course, I would recommend a Pierre de Roche. This wine is soft, and long in the palate. Also, if I may make this observation, Sir, the wine has woody and warm notes."

Rowney smiled.

"Very good, Banister. Naturally, I'd have recommended exactly the same. Do we have enough of it?"

His gaze wandered searchingly along the shelves.

Banisher cleared his throat. "Well, Sir, the Pierre de

Roche rests back here. If I am not mistaken, we should have a good ten bottles left."

Banister marched past four racks and carefully lifted a bottle from the shelf. He handed it to Rowney.

Rowney quickly glanced at it, nodded happily, and pulled a corkscrew from his pocket. Shortly thereafter he sniffed the open bottleneck, lifted it and took a healthy sip.

"Yes, that's very good. We'll take this one. Will nine bottles be enough? What do you think, Banister?"

The butler nodded. "Nine bottles seemed quite generous for eight people, Sir."

"Good. That's settled. Carry the wine upstairs now. Have our guests arrived yet?"

Banister nodded a second time.

"Yes, Sir. His lordship has arrived presently. They moved into the Queen Victoria room in the west wing. And Arthur Smith and his daughter, Meril, have the King George Suite right next door."

"Ah, the little Smith is there. Make sure she has everything. I already look forward to hearing her play. She promised me to give a small private concert on the grand piano here today."

"That will surely be delightful," commented Bannister. "As far as I know she already plays in the best houses."

"Yes, truly a talent of the century," smiled Rowney, his eyes dreamy. "And what about Ted McDonald? Did he arrive too?"

"Certainly, Sir. Mr. Ted McDonald stays in the Heinrich VIII room, right next to your daughter, Susan."

"Then everyone we invited is here," commented Carl Rowney contentedly and headed for the old armchair in front of one of the heavy oak wine racks. Here the individual owners of the castle had sat and withdrawn from the world for more than a hundred years. "I'm going to take a little nap now. Later

I'd love my daily apricot cake. And take the dog with you, yes?"

The attorney, Arthur Smith, was about to store his clothes in the large wardrobe of the King George Suite when his cellphone rang. Meril, who was also unpacking, made a face.

"You know I'm not just here for pleasure," said Arthur mildly.

He walked into the adjacent room and answered his phone.

Meril quietly slinked behind him and eavesdropped at the door.

"Of course, I've prepared everything as promised," she heard her father say. "What, now? All right, I'll come in fifteen minutes."

Arthur hung up and returned.

Meril was barely able to jump on the bed and pretend to read.

"I've got to go to the library for a minute," said the attorney to his daughter and removed his briefcase from the wardrobe. "It won't take long."

Then he patted her head and left the room.

Meril remained equally baffled and angry. She asked herself how long he was going to continue lying to her.

Carol had slipped on a very warm winter jacket and now stood at the edge of the pond right behind the castle. She could clearly smell that it would snow soon. Suddenly she heard a noise behind her. Lady Marjorie Ashtenburry approached across the wide-open space.

"Hello, Carol. Nice to see you out here. I urgently need to discuss something with you. Do you have a moment?"

Carol looked up surprised. "Of course, shall we walk a bit?"

Banister entered the kitchen in the early afternoon. Erwin followed him and ran unerringly to the large table beneath the window. On top stood, like always around this time, a plate with a piece of apricot cake for Mr. Rowney. Erwin took position in front of the plate and unmistakably barked twice.

"Oh, good boy," said the butler, "you like it too, right?"

His gaze wandered to the sideboard where the rest of the cake sat on a large baking sheet. There were at least twelve more pieces.

"You know what?" said Banister and removed the cake meant for Mr. Rowney from the plate. "This one is for us."

He took a bite and gave the rest to Erwin who excitedly wagged his tail.

Afterwards the butler took a new piece from the baking sheet and arranged it on the plate meant for Romney.

Susan stood in the onsite chapel. She gazed around deeply moved. Her breath quickened—this place was full of memories. More than eighteen years ago, as an exchange student, she'd often come here. She sank onto the first wooden bench up front. The Mother of God still smiled above the small altar, adorned with fresh flowers. Susan checked her watch. Would he come? She shivered as she noticed the air moving from the entry door. Then she turned and literally flew into his arms.

In the large dining hall precious crystal glasses and real silver cutlery sparkled in competition. Banister took great pride in classy hospitality. He'd requested the table be set with their best china and lit all the candles in the large chandeliers. The fireplace burned as well and the flames warmed the room in a comfortable manner.

After all guests had taken their seats, Mrs. McCloster served the soup and poured the sparkling wine.

"Where is Banister," asked Rowney surprised.

"He is quite embarrassed," said Mrs. McCloster, "but he is ill. Very ill!"

"Sick? What's wrong with him?" Susan's voice was filled with real worry.

"Well, some sudden nausea combined with stomach cramps. Doctor Snow was already here to give him medication. We did all we could. He very much regrets, he will not be able to serve tonight."

"Does anybody know where the dog is?" asked Carol. "I haven't seen him since this afternoon."

Rowney looked up.

"Erwin? He was in the wine cellar last and accompanied Banister upstairs. I assume he's roaming the property."

Rowney took his glass, lifted it high, and began to speak.

"I'm happy you're all here. Let us now eat. After dinner, our dear guest, Miss Meril Smith, will give us a small taste of her genius in the music room. You may look forward to a piano concert."

A murmur traveled through the dining hall and Susan, Carol and Lady Ashtenburry spontaneously applauded with enthusiasm.

"You're certainly already a much celebrated talent," said Susan. "I look forward to hearing you play!"

Meril smiled shyly as her cheeks turned red.

"After midnight I've got two more surprises for you," announced Carl.

"Really? Two surprises?" Susan looked at her father in amazement. "What do you mean?"

"You'll see later," explained Carl. "Be assured that it

will be something fantastic, especially for you." He toasted to the group. "All right, now let's eat."

At the end of the table, Lord Ashtenburry lifted his glass with the sparkling wine and scrutinized it against the candlelight. In deep concentration he took a first and then a second sip.

"Very good, very good," he said with closed lids. "Plum, licorice, and a touch of white pepper…that has to be the Shiraz."

His eyes sparkled as he spoke the words.

"You can taste that?" asked Carl Rowney. His amazement was clearly noticeable.

"Of course. This aroma is unmistakable. I bought it at auction in 2009."

"My husband is a great wine connoisseur," explained Marjorie and turned toward Carol who sat next to her. "I believe he can determine every wine in the cellar."

"I don't believe it," countered Rowney angrily. He smacked the napkin on the table.

"Oh, Papa is offended because somebody else can do something he can't," whispered Susan amused and winked at Meril who'd taken the seat next to her. "Now he'll want to chance it, you want to bet?"

"Mrs. McCloster, fetch the red wine!" grumbled Rowney as he looked at Ashtenburry provocatively.

"Carl," called Carol, "we haven't finished the soup yet. The red wine will be served with the game."

"I want to know this. Now!" declared Rowney. He unmistakably signaled Mrs. McCloster.

The red wine was delivered in a decanter and shortly after glittered in Ashtenburry's glas.

The Lord took the glass and again held it against the light. He pivoted it briefly and watched the legs the wine left inside the glass. Then he pulled it up close to his nose, stuck his nose inside the glass and took a deep breath. He repeated this process twice before he took a healthy swig.

He kept the wine on his tongue for a good ten seconds, swished the precious grape juice at first to the right, then left, pursed his lips several times…Then he swallowed and sat back with a smile on his face.

"The wine is soft, long on the palate and has woodsy and warm notes. It is the Pierre de Roche."

For a moment nobody spoke.

Then Rowney straightened and moved next to Ashtenburry.

"Did Banister give you a hint?"

"But no. How could he have known that the conversation tonight would move to this wine? I am pretty sure that I can recognize and name each of my, excuse me, your wines."

"No way, I disagree," yelled Rowney.

"Don't shout like that," scolded Carol. "We have guests and I'd like to finish this meal in peace to the end. Just like every one else, Carl."

"Well," said Lord Ashtenburry pleasantly, "We could wager a bet. We English very much love to bet."

"What for?" asked Rowney as he lit a cigarette.

"For Linley Castle?"

At once the room turned utterly silent. Carol put down her spoon and starred at her husband.

"For the castle?" whispered Rowney hoarsely.

"Yes, why not," said the Lord cheerfully and took a spoon of soup. He smiled into the group and encountered lots of horrified faces. Only Meril appeared to listen relaxed, even amused.

Rowney paced up and down behind Ashtenburry. "So you think you can recognize and name every bottle of wine stored in the wine cellar?"

"I would certainly feel confident. Yes!" declared Ashtenburry and took another spoon of soup.

"Dad, stop this nonsense and sit down again! You don't seriously want to wager the castle?" Susan glared at her father.

He simply ignored her.

"What will you wager against it, Ashtenburry? Will you offer the money, you received from me for all this?"

"Oh, I am sorry. The five million dollars more or less covered the repayment of the loans," explained Ashtenburry. "But I could offer the Rolls Royce."

"No!" Marjorie looked up appalled. "The car. You know how much I value it."

"The old pile of junk outside?" Ted got up and looked out the window. "That thing is really worth nothing."

"Shut your mouth, Ted," grumbled Carl. "I already wanted that car when we bought the castle. But your lordship didn't want to let it go. Not even for another 100,000 dollar."

"You offered 100,000 dollars for that car? That thing is ancient. What is so valuable about it?" Aghast, Susan stared at her father.

"This Rolls once belonged to the Windsors. Queen Elizabeth II and Prince Philip drove in this particular vehicle to the wedding of Charles and Diana. It means a lot to us!" explained Marjorie who was truly close to tears.

"Did you attend the wedding?" Carol looked wide-eyed at Marjorie.

"Of course," said Marjorie puzzled. "Of course, we were there, just like the entire British aristocracy!"

"All right, the bet is on," said Rowney, extending a hand to Ashtenburry.

"George, please, the car…" Marjorie implored her husband.

The Lord ignored the hand, elegantly dabbed his mouth with the napkin and stood up.

"Shall we at first determine the rules? You select a random wine from the cellar. Naturally, it has to be clear that it is one of the wines stored here at the time you purchased the castle."

"That goes without saying," said Rowney, "I haven't bought anything new yet. The cellar is still full." He took a deep drag from his cigar and continued. "If you win, you'll get back the damn castle. Arthur here is an attorney, he'll arrange everything. If I win, I'll call a cab for your home journey. The Rolls Royce will remain here...tonight."

The men eyed each other gravely and then shook hands.

"Agreed!" said Lord Ashtenburry.

"Agreed!" declared Rowney and chewed his cigar with a confident smile on his lips. He rounded the group and again sat down at the head of the table.

"So that you don't accuse me later that I snooped in the cellar, I suggest that I shall move into the library and wait there for your choice while you select the wine," said the Lord and took another sip of sparkling wine.

"Very good, Ashtenburry. I see you're a man of honor. That's exactly what I wanted to suggest. After all, I want to make sure you don't talk to anybody. That's all I need...you getting a hint or something."

Ashtenburry smiled generously. "Of course. I will read something while you select the wine. And a cup of tea with it would be marvelous."

"Why not," mumbled Rowney. "And the library will be locked. Arthur will get the key. He is an attorney and will keep it safe. And now let us eat—the soup is nearly cold."

Should you serve a menu, you can take a break here and serve the next course. Please read the remainder of the general text afterwards.

After dinner Lord Ashtenburry was accompanied by the group along the lengthy walkway from the dining hall to the library. Mrs. McCloster, carrying a tray with a cup of tea and a piece of apricot cake, led the way. The others followed, excitedly chatting at a short distance.

After arriving in the library, the Lord stepped to one of the bookshelves and selected a tome. With it he took a seat in a comfortable armchair at the window. Mrs. McCloster served the tea and apricot cake on an adjacent sidetable.

"It won't take long," explained Arthur to his friend, George, glancing at this watch. "It's now 10:50 pm. At 11:30 pm I'll rescue you."

He left the libray along with the other guests, locked the door and pocketed the key.

"We'll meet at 11:30 pm in the dining hall," said Arthur Smith to the group. "That's in a half hour." He turned to Carl. "Is that enough time to select the wine?"

Rowney smiled. "Of course that's enough time. I only need to reach into one of the wine shelves. Did Erwin come back yet?"

At 11:30pm Arthur Smith unlocked the library. Lord Ashtenburry set aside his book. "Are we ready?" asked the Lord.

"Yes, George. Now all depends on you!"

Shortly after, the two entered the dining hall together where Carol, Susan, Ted, Meril and Lady Ashtenburry were already assembled.

"Well, where is the host and the splendid wine?" asked

Arthur as he looked at Carol.

She appeared upset. "No idea, he probably fell asleep in the wine cellar. The old armchair is there. He often sleeps in it all evening."

"Good, then I'll see what he is up to," said Arthur.

He left the room, and returned to the dining hall minutes later pale as a ghost. "Something happened," he said with a shaky voice. His gaze searched for Carol. "I'm so sorry, Carol. I'm afraid, we have to call Scotland Yard."

"Why, what's the matter?"

Carol jumped up and headed for Arthur.

Arthur hesitated for a moment. Then he said in a firm voice, "Carl is dead! He…is lying in the wine cellar."

Half an hour later Scotland Yard arrived on site and, reassembling in the dining hall of Linley Castle, the group set to resolve Carl Rowney's death.

At this time, an additional explanation to accompany the story should be provided to your guests. Soon, during the introductory round, the National Trust will be mentioned. The National Trust is a nonprofit organization that stewards objects such as the preservation of historic monuments and the protection of wildlife in England, Wales and Northern Ireland.

Hannibal Winter, Inspector
Please read this introductory text to the group in first place.

Carl Rowney was bludgeoned to death with a bottle of wine. He was lying dead on an armchair in the wine cellar. He died between 11 pm and 11:30 pm. We have reason to believe that there have been two attacks on his life today.

Searching the property, our associates have found Mr. Rowney's dead German shepherd. He died from poisoning. And the police doctor has just determined that Mr. Banister, the house butler, is also suffering from poisoning. Mr. Banister has testified from his sick bed that he shared a piece of apricot cake with the dog. It wasn't exactly shared—for that Mr. Banister is quite thankful. He only took one bite and gave the rest to the dog.

Since this piece was originally meant for Mr. Rowney, we must assume, that Mr. Rowney was already supposed to be poisoned earlier this afternoon. After that attempt failed, the perpetrator made another attempt and literally struck a second time.

Please tell me, what you did tonight between 11 pm and 11:30 pm and if you observed anything suspicious. Also, I'm obviously interested who has a motive to seek Mr. Rowney's death. Always remember: In most cases people kill for disappointed love, greed or also for revenge and hate.

What Inspector Winter also knows:
More information for you! You may use all this knowledge while investigating. If you're asked, you should tell the truth because you're not the killer and have nothing to fear.

Try to solve:
Who inherits from Carl Rowney?
Rowney was a billionaire. Is there a prenuptial agreement?
Who knew that he ate a piece of apricot cake daily and that it always waited for him in the kitchen?
It is also possible that you have to find two perpetrators: the poison attack and the murder in the cellar were committed by two different killers.

Banister has just testified that he saw Ted McDonald in town today. He was obviously being threatened by two rough looking characters. Banister also testified that he told Carl Rowney about his observation. Rowney had been quite upset and worried afterwards. What does this mean?

Banister mentioned during your conversation with him that he won't continue working as a butler. He'll try to become an author. How can he afford that? He isn't even 40 years old.

Listen carefully when the individual people make their testimonies.

At the end of the investigation everyone writes down privately who he suspects as the killer and afterwards we'll solve the case together.

Lord George Ashtenburry

Please read this introductory text to the group in second place.

Since I was stuck in the library during the time of the crime and only got freed after the murder, it is certainly clear that I'm excluded as the killer. We had to separate from Linley Castle in the spring. It was absolutely impossible to afford the exorbitant maintenance costs.

I would have preferrred transferring the castle to the National Trust, but after the stock market crash I needed the money from the sale. That is very regrettable and lately, I have often thought about how I could reclaim the castle without payment and still assign it to the National Trust.

The wager was the only chance and so Marjorie and I had the idea with the wine. Only because of it did we appear here tonight. With the bet, I am sure, I would have had a good chance, because I am extremely familiar with my former wine cellar. It was worth a try.

By the way, Marjorie and I would never return here. We are glad that we now live in a wonderfully warm country manor without steps. In comparison with the castle, the maintenance costs are hardly worth mentioning. We only missed Banister terribly. Unfortunately, he will discontinue his position as a butler. Otherwise, we would have asked him to work for us again. We hardly know most of the people here. However, Arthur Smith and his daughter, Meril, are truly good friends and always welcome guests in our home.

What Lord Ashtenburry also knows:

More information for you! You may use all this knowledge during the investigation. When you're asked something, you should tell the truth because you're not the killer and don't have to fear anything.

Banister was aware of the plans for the wager and had recommended the two table wines for dinner ahead of time. He also arranged that the light in the front part of the cellar was unusable. You hoped that Rowney would therefore select a wine from the rear section of the cellar. Why?

Well, because the library has a secret door behind a bookshelf which leads directly to the wine cellar and ends in the front area of the wine cellar. Rowney didn't know about it. After the library was locked, you immediately descended into the cellar, hoping to watch Rowney during the selection process.

The passageway is quite long and when you arrived in the vault around 11:15 pm, Rowney was already lying dead in his armchair. You still heard steps walking away. That was likely the murderer.
Therefore, Carl Rowney died between 11 pm and 11:10 pm. You hurried as fast as you could upstairs and were still out of breath when the library door reopened at 11:30 pm.

What is also important:
Marjorie and Arthur Smith are somehow connected. You don't exactly know what it is, but you just sense that the two have been sharing a secret for many years. As a young girl, Susan spent a year as an exchange student with you. She stayed nearly eleven months and left abruptly without saying good-bye to you. Today is the first day you've seen her again. Back

then you always had the impression that she was in love with Banister. He was also young back then and a very good-looking fellow. You are surprised that Banister wants to quit his job. How can he afford that? Has he somehow gotten money?

A few months ago a highly reputed music boarding school inquired, if you would be willing to sponsor another master pupil. You found out that way that Marjorie spent about 100,000 dollars on Meril's piano schooling. You are speechless. Where did Majorie get so much money and why did she assume the costs for Meril's education?

And:
Of course, the Queen drives a Bentley and never a Rolls Royce. And you did also not attend the wedding of Charles and Diana—Marjorie came up with that idea to make the Rolls interesting and desirable for Rowney.

At the end of the investigation everyone writes down privately who he suspects as the killer and afterwards we'll solve the case together.

Lady Marjorie Ashtenburry
Please read this introductory text to the group in third place.

After my husband was locked in the library, I went to check on Banister. He is really quite ill, the poor fellow. I wished him a speedy recovery and exchanged a few pleasantries. Afterwards I searched for the dog—after all, he had disappeared without a trace. And because I'm a passionate animal lover, I was quite concerned.

I don't have a reason to attack Carl Rowney, though I have to say: He deserved serious punishment for the removal of the water fountain. I suppose one could call him a philistine.

What else could be important for you?
Eighteen years ago, Rowney's daughter, Susan, was a guest at our castle for nearly one year. It was a sort of student exchange, organized by the countrywomen of Kent. Today was the first time I've seen Susan since, though we had communicated via telephone several times over the years. That is how the Rowneys found out that the castle was for sale.

I don't know Mr. Ted McDonald and until today I only met Carol and Carl superficially. The attorney, Arthur Smith, has been our good friend for years and we've grown quite fond of his daughter, Meril. She had been playing piano at the castle even when she was a little girl and her talent was absolutely worth sponsoring.

I'm afraid, I shall not be able to contribute to solving this murder case.

What Marjorie also knows:
More information for you! You may use all this knowledge while investigating. If you're asked, you should tell the truth because you're not the killer and have nothing to worry about.

A good ten months after her arrival, Susan gave birth to a little girl here in the castle. At the time she was quite pudgy, therefore, the pregnancy didn't attract any attention. Back then, George was traveling. So you called the U.S. and asked Carl Rowney what he wanted you to do. At the time, Rowney was in the process of running for governor and was in the middle of the election. He explained to you that his daughter had no business to return home with a baby. You were supposed to get rid of the child and send Susan home at once. He also forbade you to share this information with anyone. For your silence he transferred 100,000 dollars to you.

You didn't hand the baby to child services, but took it to Arthur and Beth Smith. Being childless, they adopted and named the baby Meril. As an attorney Arthur was well connected and so he was able to avoid the usual dealing with the authorities. You invested the entire sum of hush money into Meril's piano education.

George never found out about it and even Meril has no idea she is adopted. For years, Susan has nagged you during your phone calls and also today in person. Susan wants to finally know where her daughter is.

Since you didn't know what to do, you finally brought her mother, Carol, into the loop today during a stroll, telling her about the birth years ago. You didn't tell her, however, that Meril is the child in question. Carol didn't know any of this and was utterly horrified. She found it even worse, how Carl acted back then. She wanted to question him immediately. Did she do it?

George was completely out of breath as he exited the library at 11:30 pm. How is that possible if he had only read? Did he perhaps use the secret hallway that leads from the library down to the wine cellar?

Of course, the Queen drives a Bentley and never a Rolls Royce. You did not attend the wedding of Charles and Diana— you came up with that idea to make the Rolls more interesting and desirable for Rowney.

At the end of the investigation everyone writes down privately who he suspects as the killer and afterwards we'll solve the case together.

Susan Rowney

Please read this introductory text to the group in fourth place.

At the time of the murder I was in my bedroom. Therefore, I've got no definite alibi. However, I did hear the water pipes in Ted's room—he stays right next to my room. I think he was taking a shower or something.

Carl was no perfect father. For him only the company and his precious reputation existed. That was all he cared about. Also he valued everything representing status. That he'd wanted the Rolls Royce only because the royal family drove in it is typical.

Eighteen years ago, he ran for governor. He sent me away from the U.S. for the election year because he worried I, being a teenager, would make some mistake that would hurt his career in politics. That's why I spent a good ten months here at the castle with Lord and Lady Ashtenburry. In the following years I often spoke with Lady Ashtenburry over the phone. But this is the first time I've returned here in person. Normally I live in the U.S. and work in our firm.

Maybe I'll stay here in England for good, because today I found out that my father wanted to nominate this Ted McDonald as his successor in our company's management. That is truly unbelievable. Until now, none of us knew Ted and I ask myself, what that's supposed to mean. Father told me he'd explain everything tonight. In addition, he personally promised me a huge surprise for midnight. Unfortunately, I won't find out now what it was all about.

What Susan also knows:
More information for you! You may use all this knowledge while investigating. If you're asked, you should tell the truth because you're not the killer and have nothing to worry about.

You spent a year here as an exchange student and fell in love with Banister. Shortly before your return to the U.S., you secretly gave birth to his/a baby (girl). You confided in Lady Marjorie. She called your father, who was in the middle of a governor's election. He was terribly worried about his reputation and forbade you to tell anybody about it or even worse, return home with the child. Lady Marjorie took the baby away and you never saw it again.

You found out from an inquiry with child services today that no child was ever dropped off during that specific timeframe. Knowing this, you confronted Lady Marjorie, but she doggedly remained silent.
Where is your daughter?

Today you met Banister again in the chapel. Banister knew nothing about the baby until now, nor did your mother. Today you told him everything. Together, you want to try finding your daughter and begin a new life together. Therefore, Banister doesn't want to continue working as a butler. You have enough money.

This afternoon you saw your mother return from the cellar. She carried a canister in her hand. What was inside the canister? You know that your parents have a prenuptial agreement. If you mother should file for divorce, she'll receive a very trivial settlement.

Today a coworker called you from the U.S. to tell you that this

Ted is supposed to take over the company's management.

Important: Just a little while ago, your father had a serious quarrel with Ted. This you heard when you passed by your father's office. What was the argument about?

At the end of the investigation everyone writes down privately who he suspects as the killer and afterwards we'll solve the case together.

Carol Rowney
Please read this introductory text to the group in fifth place.

I'm not intending to play the grieving widow here. Carl was an icecold bastard, ruthless and egotistical. The worst part was when he ran for governor eighteen years ago and sent Susan abroad. He was panicking, worried that she, being a teenager, could make a mistake and damage his reputation as a goody-two-shoes. I'm glad he lost the election at the time, otherwise life would've been unbearable with him.

After Susan's return from England ten months later, she'd grown up. She was different when she came home—quiet, pensive and she often appeared far away.
But back to Carl: Six weeks ago, he was back in the U.S. again to settle several things in the company. He returned in a strangely good mood. I asked him several times for the reasons, but he evaded my questions. Apparently, something made him very happy.

When the Lord was locked inside the library, I returned to the kitchen to check on the dessert. I heard Meril play in the music room. She played Mozart's Serenade Nr. 13. Meril is just wonderful.

What Carol also knows:

More information for you! You may use all this knowledge during this round of investigating.

For a while now you've had an affair with Arthur, the attorney. But until now a divorce was not an option, because you have a horrid prenuptial agreement and would walk away with almost nothing if you leave Carl.

Today you changed your mind because:
Lady Ashtenburry told you during your stroll that Susan gave birth to a child when she stayed at Linley Castle years ago. Carl had been informed and forbade you to tell anybody. He didn't want Susan to return home with a child because he couldn't afford a scandal during the election year. That's why Lady Ashtenburry took the baby to child services and passed it off as an orphan. At last you have an explanation for Susan's changed demeanor after her return from England.

You were shocked and confronted Carl with the news this afternoon. You told him that you're getting a divorce. He immediately agreed and also told you that Ted McDonald is his son and that he, Carl, will adopt him. You were beside yourself with fury and hate for your husband. That's why you sprinkled rat poison from the cellar on the apricot cake that is always available in the kitchen for Carl. You didn't attempt murder a second time. Therefore, you're not our main killer. However, now that Carl is dead, you'll inherit half of his estate. That's what is called motive and you'll certainly arouse suspicion.

You can divert from yourself as a suspect as follows:
Who is the father of your grandchild? Is it possible that Lord Ashtenburry…? This could certainly be the case.

And where is the child today? It's supposed to be a girl.

Banister told you in the early evening he wouldn't continue working for you. He is truly fed up working for such an unrefined man as Carl. You understand this well, but you are wondering how Banister can afford it. Can somebody in this group provide information?

Under no circumstances should you make a confession about the poisoning.

At the end of the investigation everyone writes down privately who he suspects as the killer and afterwards we'll solve the case together.

Arthur Smith, Attorney

Please read this introductory text to the group in sixth place.

My alibi? Well, honestly I don't have one. After we parted ways, I immediately went outside and smoked a cigarette. In the distance I heard Lady Marjorie call for Erwin, the German shepherd. Does that count as an alibi? I certainly don't have a motive, right? Why should I want to kill Carl Rowney? I hardly knew him. Our business transactions connected us, nothing else. For years I've been Lord and Lady Ashtenburry's attorney and we are good friends. Meril is also on very friendly terms with the Ashtenburrys.

What else might you be interested in?
After my wife died ten years ago, Meril, my daughter, spent time in various music-oriented boardingschools. She is looking at an outstanding career as a pianist—I'm very proud of her. At the moment she is rather stubborn: She hardly talks to me and I'm somewhat at a loss. It's probably her age. Otherwise, I can't say much about this situation.

What Arthur also knows:
More information for you! You may use all this knowledge during this round of investigating.

Meril is adopted. Lady Ashtenburry brought her to you eighteen years ago—she was a day old at most. She is the daughter of Susan Rowney. Susan secretly gave birth when she was an exchange student at Linley Castle. Meril doesn't know any of this and she should remain unaware.

Today after your arrival, Carl told you, he knows that Meril is his grandchild. How he could've found out is a mystery to you. Carl announced, he'd tell Meril the truth after the concert. You were quite worried because, like most artists, Meril is very sensitive. You were furious with Carl. Now that she's looking at a remarkable career as a pianist, Rowney wanted to suddenly present her as his granddaughter. But eighteen years ago, he forbade Susan to return to the U.S. with a baby. You followed Carl to the cellar at 11 pm to plead with him once more not to tell Meril. He laughed at you and declared the truth had to come out. In a bout of rage you bludgeoned Carl Rowney to death with a wine bottle. Tonight, you are the murderer! Afterwards you ran to the front of the castle and smoked a cigarette. That's when you heard Marjorie call the dog.

Also:
You've had an affair with Carol for months. Until now Carol has rejected a divorce because she had signed a very disadvantageous prenuptial agreement. She would have received nothing if she had left Carl. But tonight she told you that she now wants to go through with the divorce. Why did she make that decision today? As a widow she'd inherit half the estate.

Lady Marjorie paid for Meril's education at the music boardingschool. In all those years that amounted to 100,000 dollars. You don't know where Marjorie acquired the money.

Carl told you six weeks ago that he has an illegitimate son and that he wants to adopt him. This son is Ted McDonald. Today, Carl called you suddenly and ordered you into the library. He told you he hired a private investigator to verify Ted's status—the adoption is on hold until the results arrive.

Ask Ted about it. Why did Carl change his mind? Did he find out something about Ted?

Under no circumstances should you make a confession—others are also suspect!

At the end of the investigation everyone writes down privately who he suspects as the killer and afterwards we'll solve the case together.

Meril Smith, Pianist Protégé
Please read introductory text to the group in seventh place.

When we separated after dinner, I went to the music room and played a little on the piano because I was supposed to do a private concert later. I played from 11 pm to about 11:20 pm. Maybe somebody heard it, then I'll at least have an acoustic alibi. Afterwards I went upstairs to freshen up a bit.

At 11:30 pm I returned to the dining hall like everyone else. I've been acquainted with the castle since my childhood. Even after the sale I was back a few times. I really liked Carl Rowney—he was a super guy. Just fourteen days ago we had a longer conversation and he asked me afterwards to play this little concert here. I was happy to do it because Carl was a great listener and friend.
That's about all I can say about this.

What Meril also knows:
More information for you! You may use all this knowledge while investigating. If you're asked, you should tell the truth because you're not the killer and have nothing to worry about.

A good three weeks ago, you by chance found your birth certificate. That's how you learned you are adopted. The birthplace was registered as Linley Castle, the child listed as an orphan. Why did your father never tell you? You haven't asked him about it yet and expect that he'll tell you the truth. And who are your real parents? Please don't mention the subject to the group on your own. Wait until one of the other people confronts you with it.

Then you can surprise the others that you already knew.

During a visit here at the castle two weeks ago, you confided in Carl Rowney about your discovery. Carl reacted with a lot of understanding and promised to tell nobody. Afterwards you had the feeling that Carl knows something about your background, but didn't want to say anything about it.

Your father, Arthur, is having an affair with Carol. You know that because you've seen the two of them together in London several times. Your father has kept this secret as well. Why?

Years ago during a visit here at the castle, Banister showed you a secret passageway. It leads directly from the library to the wine cellar. Obviously, the Lord is dishonest when he says that he was locked in. He could go the wine cellar any time. The secret passage way is located behind a bookshelf.
You can certainly mention this soon because it may be important. It's clear the Lord has no alibi. You should share this as well.

The Queen has never driven in a Rolls Royce, but always a Bentley and the Ashtenburrys most certainly did not attend the wedding of Charles and Diana. His lordship seems to bend the truth quite a bit. You may want to mention this too.

At the end of the investigation everyone writes down privately who he suspects as the killer and afterwards we'll solve the case together.

Ted McDonald
Please read this introductory text to the group in eighth place.

I don't need an alibi and you'll soon understand, why. I'm really the last person to be interested in seeing Carl Rowney dead, because Carl Rowney was my father. Twenty-nine years ago he had an affair with my mother. She was his secretary back then. After her death I found documents that showed Carl Rowney was definitely my father. At last I understood why my mother never worked and she could afford to finance the most expensive schools and the best education for me. Carl paid for everything.

Six weeks ago I visited Carl in the U.S. and told him who I am. He was ecstatic to finally get to know me and invited me here to Linley Castle so that I can at last meet my half sister, Susan. Furthermore, he wanted to adopt me in a few days.

That was likely one of the surprises, Carl planned to announce after midnight. You see I would've profited from a living Carl Rowney, since I hadn't been adopted yet.
I hope Susan is happy to gain a brother.

I'm supposed to take over the management of the company. That was arranged with Carl and we already signed the required employment contracts. I need a capable assistant who'll help me get situated in the company. Susan is certainly the right person for the job.

What Ted also knows:
More information for you! You may use all this knowledge while investigating. If you're asked, you should tell the truth because you're not the killer and have nothing to worry about.

Immediately after the dinner, about 11 pm, you went to your room. Since you were freezing cold, you took a hot shower. The castle is really not heated well. Of course, you'll also inherit without an adoption, because you can confirm your parentage with DNA. The statutory share of the estate should be several million dollar.

Carl's money is coming at the right time because unfortunately you have very high debt. You are a gambler and at the moment you are being chased by nasty thugs from Las Vegas who want to collect about 400,000 dollar from a gambling debt. These thugs have followed you here and stopped you in the village this morning to seriously threaten you.

Somehow, Carl has found out about it. He questioned you today and told you, that you won't see a cent from him unless you have a one hundred percent clean record.
The adoption plans he wanted to announce today, are now supposed to be put on hold until the background check a private investigator is conducting is complete. You two had a serious argument about it in his office today. He even wanted to postpone the management leadership position until the PI's report was delivered. Nonetheless, he planned to introduce you as his son after midnight. That was one of his proclaimed surprises.

Susan was with Banister, the butler, in the small chapel. You saw them exit together—they seemed strangely acquainted, almost as if they were a couple. The billionaire's daughter and the butler? Is that possible?

When Lord George Ashtenburry was "released" from the library around 11:30 pm, he appeared strangely out of breath. This is quite odd if he only read. Make sure you question him about it.

At the end of the investigation everyone writes down privately who he suspects as the killer and afterwards we'll solve the case together.

Mrs. Vinni McCloster, Cook

Please read this introductory text to the group in ninth place.

I've been cooking here at the castle for more than twenty years. Naturally, nothing is like it was since the Ashtenburrys left. But I'm not unhappy. At least Mr. Rowney pays a higher salary. That was likely the reason why Banister had stayed here.

Eighteen years ago I took care of Susan who was visiting us for a year. Though back then, Susan was a very chubby young lady. She has very much changed for the better. Susan left some time before the year was over. I was quite sorry to see her go because Susan had really brightened our lives at the castle.

I can't contribute much else to the case, because I spend most of the time in the kitchen. And then I also had to serve dinner. With all this work one sees nothing at all.

What Mrs. McCloster also knows:

More information for you! You may use all this knowledge while investigating. If you're asked, you should tell the truth because you're not the killer and have nothing to worry about.

Mr. Rowney receives a daily apricot cake—he's quite crazy about it.

The marriage of the Rowneys is on shaky ground. Carol and Carl don't seem to have much to say to each other anymore.

Ted McDonald keeps questionable company, that's what Banister told you.

Listen carefully what the others say. Since you have a guest part, you're not under suspicion and can pay attention and draw your conclusions without distraction.

At the end of the investigation everyone writes down privately who he suspects as the killer and afterwards we'll solve the case together.

Sergeant David Mulley
Please read introductory text to the group in tenth place.

I am the assistant of Inspector Winter and sort of investigate alongside. Please contact us any time if you know anything. Thank you.

What David Mulley also knows:
More information for you! You may use all this knowledge while investigating. If you're asked, you should tell the truth because you're not the killer and have nothing to worry about.

You should note all important facts that are being investigated tonight. Believe me, with this much information, half the insights get lost. At the end you can draw the right conclusions or read aloud again what you found out.
The inspector will be impressed and you'll certainly see a promotion soon.

At the end of the investigation everyone writes down privately who he suspects as the killer and afterwards we'll solve the case together.

Testimony Neutral Observer

Please read this introductory text to the group last.

I'm participating as a neutral and independent observer in this round of investigation. Since I'm not as self-conscious as the others at the table, this is an advantage allowing me to listen closely and pay attention.

Therefore, the murderer should be prepared that I'm the person he must worry about the most. I'll pay very close attention what each person testifies and I'm sure that I'll track down the killer.

Recommendations Neutral Observer

More information for you! You may use all this knowledge while investigating. If you're asked, you should tell the truth because you're not the killer and have nothing to worry about.

At first sight you may think that having no individual part could be boring. That is not at all the case, because you are the only person in this group who has a clear conscience and doesn't have to be preoccupied with your own motives and potentially 'covering up.'

Some of the people who are sitting at this table have smaller or larger secrets—and these secrets you're going to find out. Opportunities to investigate are often overshadowed by new accusations that make people forget what was said prior. Listen closely and try to get to the root of each statement. Take notes of things you deem important.

Be prepared that you could be a suspect alone by being present. Defend yourself vigorously because you didn't do anything. Think of an excuse why you heard about the murder anyway. Why were you at the location? Who told you? Team up with one of the suspects and defend him/her vehemently. Only choose somebody you yourself exclude as the perpetrator!

Consider: Most murders are relationship crimes and happen because of jealousy or spurned love. But greed cannot be underestimated as a powerful motivator either. The important point today is this: Who had motive to commit this murder and who had the opportunity?

At the end of the investigation everyone writes down privately who he suspects as the killer and afterwards we'll solve the case together.

Resolution

Are we looking for one or two killers tonight? As we learned, Erwin, the German shepherd, was the victim of a poison attack. Banister was very lucky to survive—one more bite from the apricot cake may have led to his death. Rowney, for whom the cake was prepared daily, survived this first attempt by coincidence and later died between 11 pm and 11:30 pm from a blow to the head.

Let us first consider the poison attack:
Who knew about the daily apricot cake habit?
These are Carl Rowney himself, Mrs. Carol Rowney, Banister and Mrs. McCloster, the cook.

All others are guests and don't live permanently in the castle. Likely, Rowney wouldn't have poisoned himself and Banister certainly not—otherwise he would hardly have taken a bite. That leaves the cook and the wife, Mrs. Carol Rowney. There is no doubt that she wanted to poison her husband. We'll address motive in a moment, but generally we must ask: Did she also sneak into the basement to slay her husband?

What we should investigate tonight:

Lord Ashtenburry:
Supposedly, the Lord sat in the library during the attack. A secret hallway exists, leading from the library to the wine cellar which ends in the back part of the cellar. He took this route and arrived around 11:15 pm in the wine cellar. He hoped to be able to watch Rowney during the selection of a wine. Banister took care earlier that the light was defective in the front of the vault—the men assumed that Rowney wouldn't search around in the dark to make his selection.

Ashtenburry says Rowney was already dead and he heard steps receding. These steps likely belonged to the murderer. Provided we believe him, we can now narrow down the time of the crime. The murderer struck between 11 pm and 11:15 pm.

The Lord had no motive. He wanted to win back the castle for the National Trust. Why should he have killed Rowney?

Lady Ashtenburry:
Eighteen years ago, Lady Ashtenburry carried away Susan's baby on order from Carl Rowney. Arthur and Beth Smith named the child Meril and raised her lovingly.

Back then Carl Rowney bribed the Lady with 100,000 dollars hush money. She invested the entire amount in Meril's piano education. All these years the Lord knew nothing about it.

This afternoon, at the lake, Lady Ashtenburry filled in clueless Carol Rowney about what happened all those years ago. The Lady does not have a motive to kill Carl Rowney. She also wanted to win back the castle for the National Trust. And she has an alibi. She says she visited Banister on his sickbed around 11 pm and then later searched for the dog in the park. If we assume that visiting with sick Banister took a good ten minutes, she arrived in the park around 11:15 pm. Therefore, she was with Banister during the time of the crime.

Susan Rowney:
Eighteen years ago, Susan was here at the castle as an exchange student. She gave birth to a child. By now you know that this child is Meril. She met Banister, the father of the child, in the chapel this afternoon. Today, at last, she told Banister about the baby. As a young woman she was rather overweight, that's why nobody noticed her pregnancy.

Susan found out that the utterly unknown Ted McDonald was supposed to take over the company's management. She only learned that Ted is also her half brother during the investigation here today. Even if we assume that Ted's emergence may be a motive for Susan, we must ascertain: Susan has an alibi.

She says she was in her room between 11 pm and 11:30 pm. But she does state that she heard water running in Ted's room.

Carol Rowney:
Carol potentially has several motives.
She learned today that years ago her husband prevented Susan from bringing her baby home. Susan, who was a changed woman after her stay in England, had to live without her child for eighteen years. She herself didn't see her grandchild grow up...and all of this only because of the election year in the U.S. It's a small wonder that Mrs. Rowney was more than furious about her husband.

In addition, she also learned today that her husband has an illegitimate son. This Ted is thirty years old and that means, he was conceived with the secretary during their marriage.
Carol also has an affair with Arthur Smith. Because of a nasty prenuptial agreement she would've received not one cent had she divorced him. Today, Carol elected rat poison and contaminated the apricot cake.

However, during the time of murder she was in the kitchen and heard Meril play piano in the adjacent music room. Accordingly, Carol can be excluded as the murderer of her husband.

Ted McDonald:
Of course, Ted also has a motive because he inherits even without the adoption. He can prove with DNA that Carl is his father. The mandatory bequest alone will be in the millions. This he can really use because Ted has gambling debt and a couple of truly brutal thugs have followed him here to England. Banister watched him with these men and told Mr. Rowney about it. Afterwards, Rowney stopped the adoption. He had an argument with Ted because of these developments—a fight Susan overheard.

But Ted also has an alibi. At the time of the crime he was taking a shower and Susan heard the water running next door. He couldn't assume that Susan would hear this—he would never have used the shower as a fabricated alibi.

Meril:
Meril learned two weeks ago that she is an orphan. During a conversation here in the castle two weeks ago she told Carl Rowney about this discovery. She couldn't know that she was facing her grandfather.

Meril has no motive, but an alibi. At the time of the crime she played piano—Carol heard her play from the kitchen.

Arthur Smith:
Back then, Arthur Smith along with his wife adopted baby Meril and lovingly raised her. They made Meril into the person she is today. Arthur also has an affair with Carol.

Today Carl told Arthur outright that he is Meril's grandfather. Of course, Rowney himself knew this from his conversation with Meril here in the castle two weeks prior. He told Arthur he would announce this tonight after midnight. This is also the proclaimed surprise he'd promised Susan.

He wanted to present Susan with her daughter—particularly a daughter who was looking at a brilliant career. That was something for Rowney who loved castles, German shepherds and Rolls Royces. The famous granddaughter was something he suddenly wanted for himself and his family.

Arthur was desperate and followed Rowney into the basement right after 11 pm. Because of Meril a fight ensued and Arthur slayed the Texan in a fit of rage. He then rushed to the park and overheard Lady Marjorie call after the dog.

But we know that this had to be after 11:15 pm because the Lady had visited the butler earlier. Arthur is the only one in the group who has a motive but no alibi for the time between 11 pm and 11:15 pm.
Arthur is our killer.

Closing Remarks

The applause didn't want to end. Exhausted but happy Meril straightened from her piano chair and tottered a bit clumsily a few steps toward the edge of the stage. She bowed several times and as the audience of New York Carnegie Hall stood up to applaud, she discovered her parents in the first row.

"Pinch me," whispered Susan to Thomas Banister, wiping a tear from the corner of her eye. "Somehow all this is too good to be true."

Inspector Winter and David Mulley sat in one of the large white tents that surrounded Linley Castle and drank tea.

The Inspector glanced at his watch. "Where are the Lord and Lady? In ten minutes his lordship is supposed to cut the ribbon to officially turn over the castle to the National Trust. What will we do if the Lord isn't coming?"

"Well, Sir, I think if the Lord doesn't come, Mrs. Carol Rowney will cut the ribbon. Ultimately, the trust can thank her for this generous gift."

The inspectior shook his head.

"You're not up to date, Mulley! Mrs. Rowney, along with Arthur Smith and Mr. Ted, has already left for the U.S. yesterday to arrange the estate and introduce Ted to the business. I don't have a clue who should transfer the castle if the Lord and Lady don't show.

"Well, Sir, it definitely should be somebody who has been living in the castle a long time and knows a lot about its history and occupants," commented Mulley thoughtfully.

Then his gaze fell on Vinni McCloster who was just carrying another tray of apricot cake from the kitchen, arranging it on one of the dessert buffets.

Mulley's face brightened. "I think I have found the appropriate person!"

"What in heavens *is* that?" called Lady Marjorie in a terrified voice, watching a white cloud ascend from the Rolls Royce's bonnet. The car lumbered a few more feet along the country path and came to a stop.

"Don't tell me we have car trouble, George! We are already quite late. You think it will start up again?"

The Lord disembarked wordlessly and opened the bonnet.

Marjorie cranked down the window and leaned out. "Can you see anything?"

Ashtenburry shook his head and looked at his wife.

"I'm afraid there is nothing left to do," he said. "We shall have to walk back home on foot."

"Oh, I'm dreadfully sorry about it, George. You're supposed to cut the ribbon and turn the castle over to the National Trust."

The Lord waved a hand and walked to the boot.

"You know, Marjorie," he said when he returned with two pairs of rubber boots shortly after and handed one through the window to his wife, "honestly, I was no longer that keen on cutting the ribbon, and undoubtedly the Trust will receive the castle without this spectacle or our help."

The Lady looked up at her husband in surprise and also exited the car.

"But I thought, you looked forward to transfer the castle and have it preserved. They even want to reinstall the old fountain."

"Of course, I'm happy," smiled the Lord, "but celebrations of this size are not something I'm excited about. And is a pleasant walk through the Scottish fields not a much better alternative?"

Marjorie leaned against the car and gazed around.

The angular and rustic nature of Scotland, she and

George loved so much, spread as far as the eye reached.

"You're right as usual, George!" declared the Lady and took her husband's hand. "Let's go home to our wonderfully warm land manor!"

The End

Author Bio

Cornelia H.-Müller has been an author since 2006. Her genres include murder mystery games, children's plays and theater plays.
Author contact at
glashauskrimi@glashauskrimi.de

Visit Cornelia H.-Müller at her homepage:
www.glashauskrimi.de

Additional books by the author were released in the German language by Editon Paashaas Verlag:

Entdecken Sie Ihren kriminalistischen Spürsinn!
Mithilfe dieser Bücher können Sie zu Hause gemeinsam mit Ihren Familienmitgliedern und Gästen auf Tätersuche gehen. Sie ermitteln und befragen, Sie bewerten Tatsachen und Aussagen und Sie finden schließlich heraus, wer der Täter oder die Täterin ist.

Krimiparty: 5 neue Fälle für Ihre Ermittlungen zu Hause
2. Ausgabe, April 2015,
ISBN: 978-3-9813928-8-3, 13,95 €

Diese Krimis finden Sie in dem Buch:
Irrtum oder Absicht? - Für 5-7 Spieler
Mord in bester Gesellschaft - Für 6 Spieler
Muttertag - Für 8-10 Spieler
Mann über Bord - Für 7-10 Spieler
Feine Verhältnisse! - Für 7-10 Spieler
Altersempfehlung: 12 bis 99 Jahre

Krimiparty Sonderausgabe 1:
Plötzlich und erwartet
Ein Fall mit Kommissarin Henriette Kragenberg
ISBN: 978-3-942614-25-2, 7,95 €

Karl-Friedrich von Staffelberg, ein wohlhabender Gewürzfabrikant, lädt zu einem feierlichen Weihnachtsessen ein. Zum ersten Mal ist in diesem Jahr auch Karl-Friedrichs frischangetraute dritte Ehefrau, die junge und schöne Jaqueline, dabei. Dies wäre kaum erwähnenswert, stünden nicht auch die beiden Ex-Ehefrauen des Fabrikanten, Irene und Monika, auf der Gästeliste. Zu alledem sieht sich der Gastgeber am Weihnachtsabend mit wirklich ärgerlichen Indiskretionen konfrontiert! Dennoch endet das Fest ganz harmonisch, doch am nächsten Morgen gibt es einen Toten in der Villa zu beklagen ...

Krimiparty Sonderausgabe 2:
Workshop mit Todesfolge
Ein Krimi aus dem Allgäu.
ISBN: 978-3-942614-39-9, 7,95 €

Toni Burger führt gemeinsam mit seiner Frau Zenzia einen einsam gelegenen Sennerhof inmitten des wunderschönen Allgäus.

An einem Wochenende trifft sich dort eine Reisegruppe, um mit einem Fasten- und Meditationsprogramm dem Alltag zu entfliehen. Ganz so friedlich wie die Wollschweine, die der Toni züchtet, ist die Gegend allerdings nicht, denn schon am zweiten Tag gibt es einen Toten zu beklagen.

Krimiparty Sonderausgabe 3:
Die Rache
A Thriller - für Ladies only.
ISBN: 978-3-942614-41-2, 7,95 €

Die Rache ist süß... und manchmal zartbitter!
8 Frauen treffen sich an einem Wochenende im November in dem einsam gelegenen Landhaus der schwerreichen Camilla von Strelitz. Dort, in den Highlands nahe Iverness, sorgen ein Stromausfall, ein durchgebrannter Gaul und ein Todesfall für reichlich Abwechslung. Ermitteln Sie mit, wenn wir versuchen, etwas Licht in diesen nebulösen Fall zu bringen.

Krimiparty Sonderausgabe 4:
MorgenGrauen
Ein Mitspielkrimi aus Bayern
ISBN: 978-3-942614-58-0, 7,95 €
Neuerscheinung November 2013

Lokalzeitung Wulfrathshausen:
Der Brauereibesitzer Konrad Weiblinger wurde bei einem Jagdunfall im Wulfrathshausener Forst tödlich verletzt.
Nähere Umstände zu dem tragischen Unglück sind bislang nicht bekannt. Der Unternehmer war weit über die Grenzen Bayerns hinaus bekannt und geschätzt. Besonders tragisch ist, dass Konrad Weiblinger am kommenden Montag die Münchner Immobilienhändlerin Susanne Schwammberger heiraten wollte...

Krimiparty Sonderausgabe 5:
Spargelsilvester
Ein ländlicher Krimi nicht nur zur Spargelzeit!
ISBN: 978-3-942614-71-9, 7,95 €

Harry Petterson, Spargelbauer und Besitzer von
Gut Landswede in Schleswig-Holstein, hat
großen Grund zur Sorge. Ein hässlicher
Erbstreit trübt die Stimmung in der Familie
ebenso, wie das außergewöhnliche Geschenk,
welches Hetty dem gemeinsamen Sohn Heiko
ohne jede Absprache zum 22. Geburtstag gemacht hat.
Und Tochter Syke? Sie treibt sich neuerdings auffällig oft im Heu
herum und zickt mit ihrer aus Amerika angereisten Kusine Jaba um
die Wette. Als das Spargelfest zum Saisonende für einen der
Bewohner des Hofes tödlich endet, beginnt der Alptraum für Harry
und die Seinen allerdings erst so richtig!

Krimiparty Sonderausgabe 6 - Inkognito
- ein Hotelkrimi
ISBN: 978-3-945725-12-2, 7,95 €
Neuerscheinung Februar 2015

Spitzenkoch Jaques Pampelmues steht vor
seinem größten Triumph; nachdem sein
Kochbuch „Jaques á la Carte" seit Wochen auf
den Bestsellerlisten steht, plant der
Fernsehproduzent Frank Bachhausen
jetzt eine eigene Kochshow im TV mit ihm. Man
sollte annehmen, dies seien wunderbare Nachrichten für Jaques und
seine tüchtige Frau Wanda, aber warum zickt Letztere plötzlich so
herum? Und warum checkt die Schauspielerin Vanessa Steenhagen
unter falschem Namen im Hotel Pampelmues ein? Eine Leiche in
Zimmer 223, ein Feueralarm und zwei vertauschte Koffer führen zu
weiterer Verwirrung in diesem undurchsichtigen Fall.

Krimiparty Sonderausgabe 7
Bayern-Spezial
mit 2 Fällen: MorgenGrauen + Neues aus
Wulfrathshausen
ISBN: 978-3-945725-45-0, 11,95 €

Cornelia H.-Müller präsentiert 2 Fälle aus
Bayern aus der beliebten Mitspiel-Krimi-Reihe
"Krimiparty".

- Fall 1: MorgenGrauen
- Fall 2: Neues aus Wulfrathshausen

Beide Kriminalfälle sind unabhängig voneinander spielbar.

Krimiparty Sonderausgabe 8:
Der fast perfekte Mord - ein Sylt-Krimi

Cornelia H.-Müller
ISBN: 978-3-945725-84-9, 7,95 €
Neuerscheinung September 2016

Der fast perfekte Mord - ein Sylt-Krimi.
Auch ein so traumhafter Ort wie die
wunderschöne Insel Sylt ist vor Verbrechen nicht
gefeit. Kommissar Ludger Hansen hat in diesem
Mitspielkrimi von Cornelia H.-Müller den Mord
an einem Finanzbeamten aufzuklären.

Beinahe zeitgleich zu dem Verbrechen gab es am Strand von
Hörnum einen seltsamen Unfall mit einem Schwerverletzten.
Hängen beide Fälle zusammen oder ist dies einfach nur Zufall?

Krimiparty Kids - Band 1
Kunstraub in New York
ISBN: 978-3-945725-25-2, € 7,95
Altersempfehlung: ab 12 Jahren
Mitspieler: 6 bis 7 Personen

Der Künstler Harm Airbrush wittert die Chance seines Lebens, als eine New Yorker Galeristin völlig überraschend einen Besuch in seinem Hamburger Atelier ankündigt. Sie ist allerdings nur an einem einzigen Bild interessiert und dieses verschwindet wenig später auf rätselhafte Weise. Die Ermittlungen führen unsere Mitspieler bis nach New York.
Werden sie den Kunstdieb entlarven können?
Anders als bei der beliebten Krimiparty-Reihe geht es bei *Krimiparty Kids* nicht um Mord. Daher sind diese Ermittlungen auch für ein jüngeres Publikum bestens geeignet.

Krimiparty Sonderausgabe 9: Die Wette
ISBN: 978-3-945725-98-6, 7,95 €
Neuerscheinung 12/2016

Lord Ashtenburry musste sein Anwesen, das altehrwürdige Linley-Castle, veräußern. Der neue Besitzer, ein texanischer Ölmilliardär, lädt die Ashtenburrys und weitere Gäste auf das Schloss ein. Keine leichten Zeiten für den gleich mit erworbenen Butler des Hauses. Trotzdem spricht alles für einen launigen Abend, bis es zu einer geradezu aberwitzigen Wette kommt. Noch vor Mitternacht gibt es eine Leiche und Inspector Hannibal Winter wird es nicht einfach haben, den Mord aufzuklären.
Kommen Sie mit auf das schottische Schloss und versuchen Sie, den Fall mit Ihrem Ermittlerteam zu entwirren!

Translated by Annette Oppenlander - Author Bio

Annette Oppenlander is a German-American historical novelist. When she isn't in front of her computer, she shares her knowledge through writing workshops and indulges her old mutt, Mocha. In her spare time she travels around the U.S. and Europe to discover amazing histories. The mother of three 'former' teens, Annette lives with her husband in Bloomington, Indiana, USA.

"Nearly every place holds some kind of secret, something that makes history come alive. When we scrutinize people and places closely, history is no longer a date or number, it turns into a story."

Author contact at Annette.oppenlander@yahoo.com
Visit Annette Oppenlander at her homepage:
www.annetteoppenlander.com

Books by Annette Oppenlander:
- A Different Truth
- Escape from the Past: The Duke's Wrath (Book One)
- Escape from the Past: The Kid (Book Two)
- Escape from the Past: At Witches' End (Book Three)

Upcoming: A novel I've been working on since 2002, based on the history of my family and my hometown, Solingen, Germany during and after World War II.